BOTH
PUBLISHING

'*The Stamp of a Criminal*' was first published in the collection entitled *A Twist of the Knife* by Peter James. First published in 2014 by Macmillan, an imprint of Pan Macmillan, a division of Macmillan Publishers International Limited.

Copyright © Really Scary Books/Peter James 2014.

Roy Grace® is a registered trade mark of Really Scary Books Limited.

This edition published in 2023 by BOTH Publishing under licence.

The Author has asserted his/her moral right to be identified as the author of this Work in accordance with the Copyrights, Designs and Patents Act 1988.

This book is sold subject to the condition that no part may be reproduced, distributed, or transmitted in any form or by any means, including photocopying, recording, or other electronic or mechanical methods.

A CIP catalogue record of this book is available from the British Library

ISBN - 978-1-913603-27-4

eBook available
ISBN - 978-1-913603-28-1

Distributed by BOTH Publishing.

Cover design and typeset by Chrissey Harrison. Cover images by Luciano Demarchi, gary71, Love the wind, and vvoe, licensed via Shutterstock.

Part of the Dyslexic Friendly Quick Reads Series.

www.booksonthehill.co.uk

STAMP
OF A
CRIMINAL

Peter James

Other dyslexic friendly quick read titles from BOTH publishing

Sharpe's Skirmish

Six Lights off Green Scar

Silver for Silence

Blood Toll

The Dust of the Red Rose Knight

The House on the Old Cliffs

Ultrasound Shadow

At Midnight I Will Steal Your Soul

The Clockwork Eyeball

Sherlock Holmes and the
Four Kings of Sweden

Foreword

By Peter James

Back in 2010 I wrote my first *Quick Reads* novella, THE PERFECT MURDER. This was written as adult fiction but with no long words, and was aimed at people who struggled in some way with literacy.

I was lucky enough to win the *Reader's Favourite Award*. At the reception, I was approached by a lady in her late 50s who was close to tears. She told me my novella was the first book she had ever read that was not written for children. For years she had been too embarrassed ever to read in public – on a beach, a park or a bus or a train – because the only stories she was able to cope with were children's books.

Looking at the dyslexic friendly books BOTH published last year I can see how the larger spacing between the words and larger print create an easy-to-read and accessible format without detracting from the narrative journey. I am excited to be part of their project as it is thanks to initiatives such as the work BOTH is doing, that the condition of dyslexia is now catered for in fiction, and people, such as the lady I met, can hold her head up and read in public, like so many other ordinary people.

Stamp of a Criminal

The dog was a wuss, Crafty Cunningham always said. An adorable wuss, certainly, but a wuss nonetheless.

His wife, Caroline, agreed. He was a big dog, a lot of dog, especially when he jumped on you, wet and muddy from the garden, and tried to lick your face. It was like having a sheep fall off a cliff and land on you. His name was Fluff, which was a ruddy stupid name, they both knew, for a dog of this size. The animal was still unable to grasp the fact that after eleven years (a ripe seventy-seven in dog time) he was no longer a tiny, fluffy puppy, but was a very large, overweight and usually smelly golden retriever.

They both loved him, despite the fact they had been badly advised on their choice of a puppy. They'd originally wanted a guard dog that would be happy roaming a big garden in Brighton, and wouldn't need too many walks beyond that. Fluff needed two long walks daily, which he did not often get, which was why he was overweight. And as a guard dog he was about as much use as a chocolate teapot. Crafty was fond of telling their friends that the hound might drown a burglar in slobber, but that would be about his limit.

Crafty's real name was Dennis, but he'd acquired the nickname back in his school days and it had stuck. He'd always been one for a crafty dodge. He used to play truant from school; he was a crafty dodger around the football pitch, and equally crafty at dodging trouble. And he was always one for getting something for nothing. His father had once said of him, with a kind of grudging respect, "Dennis is a lad who could follow you in through a turnstile and come out in front of you without having paid."

Neither of them heard Fluff, early that April Tuesday morning, pad upstairs from the kitchen, where he usually slept, and flop down on their bedroom floor. Later, Crafty would tell the police he thought he had heard whimpering, around 5 a.m. he estimated, but because he wasn't aware the dog was in the bedroom, he thought the sound was coming from Caroline, having a bad dream.

It was only when Crafty woke at 7 a.m., with that very distinct smell of damp dog in his nostrils, that he saw Fluff on the floor. To his surprise, the dog was shaking. "Fluff!" he hissed, not wanting to wake Caroline, who never rose before 8.30. "What are you doing here, boy?"

The dog gave him a baleful look, stood up, still shaking, padded to the door, then turned back to him and gave a single bark that was much higher than his usual.

"Ssshhhh, boy!" Crafty said, but at the same time he thought the dog was behaving in a very strange way – almost as if he was trying to tell him something. Was he ill? "Need to go out, do you? What's the matter? Why are you shaking?" he whispered, then slipped out of bed, pushed his feet in his slippers, and unhooked his silk paisley dressing gown from the back of the door. It was cold in the room and he was covered in goosebumps, he realized. Spring was meant to be here, although there was still a wintry chill in the air. But that could not be why Fluff was shaking – he had too much fur on him to be cold, surely?

The dog barked again, trotted a short way down the stairs, then turned, looked up at his master and barked again.

"You're definitely trying to tell me something, aren't you, boy?"

He was.

■ ■ ■

Detective Constable Roy Grace sat at his small desk in the detectives' room, on the second floor of Brighton's John Street police station, which was to be his home for the foreseeable future.

He put down his mug of coffee from the canteen, and removed his jacket. His desk, apart from a telephone, his radio next to it and a copy of yesterday's briefing notes, was almost bare. He opened his attaché case and pulled out a few personal belongings, and started by pinning up in front of him a photograph of his fiancée, Sandy. She was smiling, leaning against a railing on the seafront, the wind blowing her long blonde hair. Next he placed in front of him a photograph of his parents. His father, Jack, stood proudly in his uniform bearing

Sergeant stripes.

Roy had recently completed his two years as a probationer, walking the beat in Brighton as a Constable, and he had loved it. But right from his early teens he had dreamed of becoming a detective. He still could not really believe that he now was one.

This was his second day in his new role, and he loved the sound of his title. Detective Constable Grace. *Detective!* Sandy loved it too, and told him she was very proud of him. He sipped some coffee and stifled a yawn. He had been told he did not need to be in until 8 a.m., but he wanted to make a good impression – and perhaps bag an early worm – so he had arrived at the police station, in a smart blazer and slacks, at 7 a.m., hoping for a more challenging day than yesterday when, in truth, he'd felt a little bored. Wasn't this supposed to be the second busiest police station in the UK? It had felt as quiet as a mortuary.

What he needed was a case to get his teeth into. Nothing had happened on his first day, apart from attending a briefing, some basic familiarization with the routines, and being given his shifts for the three months ahead. It had been a quiet Monday generally, blamed largely on the pelting rain. "Policeman Rain" it was jokingly called, but it was true. Levels of crime fell dramatically when the weather was rubbish. Today looked better, an almost cloudless sky giving the promise of sunshine. And crime!

Yesterday, he reflected, had felt a bit

like his first day at school, getting to know the ropes and his new colleagues. There had been a handful of follow-ups from crimes committed on the Sunday night – a string of break-ins, a couple of street robberies, several motor vehicle thefts, a racist attack on a group of Asians by one of the town's nasty youth gangs, and a drugs bust on a private dwelling – but other detectives had been despatched to handle those. He had spent most of his first day chatting to colleagues, seeing what he could learn from them, and waiting for his Detective Sergeant, Bill Stoker, to give him an action; he hoped today would not be a repeat.

He did not have to wait long. The DS, a burly former boxer, ambled over, wearing a charcoal suit that looked a size too big for him and black shoes polished to a military shine. "Right, old son, need to send you out. Domestic burglary in Dyke Road Avenue. Sounds like a high value haul. I'll come with you – but I'll let you lead. I've already got SOCO on standby."

■ ■ ■

Grace hoped his excitement didn't show on his face too much. He drove the unmarked Metro up past Brighton railway station, carefully sticking to the speed limit, across the Seven Dials roundabout and on up Dyke Road, then into Dyke Road Avenue, lined on both sides with some of the town's swankiest houses.

"Not many coppers living on this street," his Sergeant observed wryly. "Not many honest ones at any rate."

There had been a big police corruption scandal some years back, which Roy Grace's father had talked about, and which had left a bad taste in everyone's mouth – police and public alike. He decided, from the Sergeant's slightly bitter tone, not to probe. Just as he was about to make a non-committal comment, his colleague said, "Here, that's it, over on the left, on that corner!"

Grace pulled over. There was a narrow driveway with in-and-out gates; both sets were open – and from their poor state of repair, it did not look as if they had been closed in years. "I think if I lived on this street, I'd keep my gates shut – open like that is an invitation," he said.

"Most people don't have a bloody clue about security," the Detective Sergeant said. "All right, before we get out of the car, what's this place tell you at first glance?"

Roy Grace stared at the house. It was secluded from the street by a wooden fence badly in need of repair, rising above which, on the other side, was a tall, neatly trimmed privet hedge. The house itself was an Edwardian mansion, with window frames that, he could see from here, looked in poor condition. "Elderly people live here," Grace said. "They've probably owned the property for several decades, and never bothered with an alarm. There's no box on the outside of the house."

The Detective Sergeant raised his eyebrows. "What makes you think the occupants are elderly?" He looked down at his notepad. "Mr and Mrs Cunningham."

"Old people get worried about money, sir. They don't like to spend anything they don't have to. So they haven't done maintenance on the exterior for a very long time. But I suspect they are keen gardeners – and they have the time, which means they are retired. Look at the condition of the hedge. It's immaculate – trimmed by a perfectionist."

"Let's see if you're right," Bill Stoker said, climbing out.

Grace looked at him. "Is there

something you know about these people that I don't?"

Stoker gave a non-committal shrug and a wry smile. The two men walked up the threadbare gravel of the driveway. An elderly Honda saloon was parked near the front door. From what they could see of the garden from their position, all the shrubbery was neatly tended, but close up, Grace could see the exterior of the house was in an even worse state of repair than he had first assessed, with large chunks of the pebbledash rendering missing and a few ominous patches of damp on the walls.

They entered the porch and rang the bell. Instantly, they heard the half-hearted bark of a dog, and a few moments later the door was opened by a wiry, energetic-looking man in his early seventies, Grace estimated. Grace shot Bill Stoker a quick glance; Stoker gave a small grin of approval.

"Mr Cunningham?"

"Yes?"

Grace pulled out his warrant card holder and flipped it open, to show his card and the Sussex Police badge. It was the first time he had used it, and he felt a deep thrill. "Detective Constable Grace and Detective Sergeant Stoker, from Brighton CID, sir. We understand you've had a break-in?"

The old man, dressed in a plaid shirt with a cravat, chinos and monogrammed velvet slippers, looked distinctly on edge and a tad lost. His hair was a little long and unkempt, giving him the air of an absent-minded professor. He did not look to Roy Grace like a man who had ever held a staid office job – possibly a former antiques dealer or someone in the arts world, perhaps. Definitely some kind of wheeler-dealer.

"Yes, that's right. Bloody awful. Thank you for coming. I'm so sorry to have troubled you."

"No trouble at all, sir," Bill Stoker said. "That's what we're here for."

"It's shaken us up, I can tell you. Please come in. My wife and I have tried to be careful not to touch anything, but the ruddy dog's trampled all over – I suppose what you fellows call – the *crime scene*."

"We'll have SOCO take some paw prints, so we can rule him out as a suspect, sir," Bill Stoker said, entering the rather grand panelled hallway. Several fine-looking oil paintings were hung along the walls, and it was furnished with tasteful antiques. He knelt to stroke the dog which had padded over towards him, tongue out. "Hello, fellow!" He rubbed the dog's chest gently. "What's your name?" he asked, looking at the collar tag. "Fluff. You're Fluff, are you?" Then he heard a female voice.

"Who is it, darling?"

"The Police. CID. Two detectives."

"Oh, thank God."

Caroline Cunningham was an elegant woman in her late sixties, with neatly coiffed hair and a face that was still handsome despite her wrinkles. She must have been very beautiful in her youth, Roy Grace thought. She was wearing a white blouse, black slacks and sparkly trainers.

Her husband introduced them, getting their names and ranks the wrong way round. Roy Grace corrected him.

"Would you gentlemen like some tea or coffee?" she asked.

Grace did fancy a coffee but was unsure it would be professional to accept. "We're fine," he said. "Thank you very much." Then he noticed the look of dismay on Bill Stoker's face. Ignoring it, he ploughed on. "I understand two officers attended an emergency call made at 7.10 a.m. today from this address, Mr and Mrs Cunningham?"

"Correct. We didn't know if the blighters... were still in the house. We were bloody terrified – and the dog was no damned use at all!"

"My husband has a shotgun, but of course it's locked away in the safe in the garage," she said.

"Probably just as well, madam," Bill Stoker said. "Once a firearm is involved, matters can turn very dangerous very quickly."

"I'd have given them both barrels and to hell with it," Crafty Cunningham said.

From the grimace on his face, Roy Grace had no doubt he meant it. "I think what would be most helpful is if you can you talk us through exactly what happened from the moment you discovered the break-in, then we'd like to go through what has been taken."

"I'm not sure we can remember exactly what's been taken – but the majority of it, certainly," the old man replied.

"Georgian silver mostly," Caroline Cunningham said. "They knew their stuff whoever did this. They didn't seem to bother with much else."

"From what you are saying, you seem pretty certain it was more

than one intruder?" Grace said.

"Damned right it was," Crafty said. "The buggers made themselves breakfast in the kitchen before they left! Two bowls of cereal, bread, butter and marmalade. Can you believe it?"

"Maybe it would be a good idea if we could sit down and go through everything," Bill Stoker said. "Then we'll take a look around afterwards. Is there a room that the… er… intruders didn't enter, to your knowledge?"

"The conservatory," Caroline Cunningham said.

"Let's go in there."

"Are you sure you wouldn't like tea or coffee?" she asked.

This time Grace looked at his Sergeant for a lead. "I wouldn't say no to a cuppa," Stoker said. "Thank you."

"A coffee for me, please," Grace said. "But I'm a bit worried, if they've been in your kitchen, about contaminating any possible evidence."

The couple looked at each other guiltily. "Erm, I'm afraid we have already been in there, and made ourselves something to eat – not that either of us had much of an appetite. But we had a feeling it was going to be a long morning," Crafty replied.

Bill Stoker looked at his watch. "Someone from SOCO should be along shortly to dust for prints. They'll need to take both of yours, to know which ones to eliminate, if that's all right?"

"Yes, indeed," Caroline Cunningham said.

"And the dog's, also?" her husband said, with a smile.

"Have you lost a lot?" Grace asked them.

"Quite a bit, in value," Crafty replied.

"Much of it sentimental. Bits and pieces I'd inherited from my parents," Caroline said. "And wedding presents. Christening cups and napkin rings. To be honest, we're pretty numb. A lot's happened in the last hour – hour and a half…" She looked at the wall, and frowned.

"No! Bastards."

Grace followed her gaze and saw a rectangular shadow on the wall.

"That was a beautiful antique French wall clock."

"Belonged to my great-grandfather," Crafty Cunningham said ruefully. "Bloody hell, what else has gone?"

"I'm afraid people often keep finding things missing for weeks after a burglary," Bill Stoker said. "Let's go and sit down and take things slowly from the beginning."

■ ■ ■

Tony Langiotti watched from his office window as the white Renault van came around the corner into the mews. His mews. He owned all eight of the lock-up garages, and the warehouse opposite. That meant no strangers with prying eyes could see who came and went. He put down his coffee, lit a cigarette, and with it dangling from his lips went outside to meet the two Welsh scumbags.

"You're fucking late. What kept you?"

he said to the van's driver, Dai Lewellyn. The Welshman was in his early twenties, with a cratered, emaciated face and a hairstyle like his mother had just tipped a bowl of spaghetti on his head. "Stop to get your toenails varnished or something?"

"We went to get breakfast," Lewellyn said cheerily, in a sing-song voice.

"We've been up since early, like, we were hungry, like," the other man, in the passenger seat said. His name was Rees Hughes. Both occupants of the van were dressed in postmen's uniforms.

Langiotti hauled up the door of garage number 4, and signalled for them to drive in. Then he switched on the interior light and pulled the door back down behind them.

They were in a large space, eight lock-up garages wide, with all the internal walls knocked down. There were two other vans in there, a machine for manufacturing number plates, a number of old vending machines stacked against the far wall, and a line of trestle tables, which gave it the faint appearance of a village hall.

"So what you tossers got for me?" The cigarette dangled from Langiotti's lips, with an inch of ash on the end.

"I don't like your tone," the fat one said in a mild rebuke, getting out of the van.

"Yeah, well, I don't like being kept waiting, see? So what you got for me?" He walked around to the rear of the van, and saw the two large grey mail sacks lying there, each stamped *GPO*.

"We did the Dyke Road Avenue House."

"Yeah? Any bother?"

"No, there was no alarm, like you said. The dog wasn't any trouble either, like you said it wouldn't be."

"I do my research," Langiotti said. "You got some good gear for me?"

Dai pulled the first sack out; it clinked as he put it down, then he untied the neck and Langiotti peered in, taking a pair of leather gloves from his pocket and pulling them on. He removed a silver Georgian fruit bowl from the sack and held it up, turning it around until he could see the hallmark. "Nice," he said. "Very nice."

"We took the Georgian silver – we identified it from the pictures you gave us from the insurance company. There was a nice-looking clock we saw that wasn't on the list, but it looked good to us."

"Anything else that wasn't on the list?"

The two Welshmen looked at each other and shook their heads.

"I wouldn't want to find out you'd nicked something that you didn't tell me about, know what I mean? That you'd kept something for yourselves, yeah? It's when people try to flog stuff on the side that trouble happens. That's how you get nicked, you know what I'm saying?"

Dai Lewellyn pointed at the two sacks. "Everything we took is in these."

Langiotti took each item out, carefully

setting it down on the trestles. Then he ran through the haul, checking each item against the insurance inventory, and jotting numbers down on his notepad. When he had finished he said, "Right, by my reckoning, I've got a market value here of forty-five thousand quid, less what I'll have to knock off. We agreed ten per cent of value, right?"

The two Welshmen nodded.

"Right, come across to my office and I'll square up, and give you tonight's address. Got a good one for you tonight, I have."

Their eyes lit up greedily.

■ ■ ■

The Cunninghams took the two detectives into the rooms where items had been stolen, making an inventory as they went. But with the couple constantly interrupting and contradicting each other, it took some time for Roy Grace and Bill Stoker to get a clear idea of the sequence of events and of what had been taken.

The dining room had been the most badly affected. Caroline Cunningham pointed out, tearfully, the bare sideboard where much of the fine silver had stood, as well as a Georgian silver fruit bowl, which, she told them, had been in her family for five generations, and had stood in the centre of the fine oval dining table.

Back in the conservatory again and sipping another cup of coffee, Grace studied his notes and asked them to go through the events of the early morning once more. Crafty Cunningham said he was roused by a whimpering sound, which he thought was his wife having a nightmare, and happened to notice on the bedside clock that it was just past 5 a.m.; then he went back to sleep. He went downstairs at 7.10 a.m. to find the burglars had broken in through the toilet window, which was along the side of the house. The glass had been cut neatly, rather than broken, which meant their entry had been almost silent. They had left via the kitchen door, which the Cunninghams had found unlocked.

Roy Grace stared out at the large, beautifully tended garden, with its swimming pool and tennis court, and did a quick calculation. The burglars had entered before sunrise. OK, it was logical for them to have broken in while it was still dark. But why at 5 a.m.? There was a risk that daylight would be breaking when they left. Why not much earlier in the night? Or was this the last of a series of houses the perpetrators were burgling last night? But if that was the case, surely the police would have heard of other burglaries by now – it was nearly 9.30 a.m.

"I don't suppose you have any idea what time the intruders might have left?" He addressed both the Cunninghams.

They shook their heads.

"What time are your newspapers delivered?"

"About a quarter to seven," Caroline Cunningham said.

"If you could give me the details of your newsagent, we'll check with the paperboy to see if he noticed anything unusual. Also, what time does your post normally arrive?"

"About 7.30 a.m.," the old man said.

"We'll check with the post office also."

Then the two detectives went back carefully over the inventory of stolen items, reading it all out to the couple and asking them several times if there was anything else that had been taken which they might have overlooked. It was clearly a big haul, and the burglars seemed to be professionals who knew exactly what they were taking.

As the Cunninghams showed the two detectives to the front door, thanking them for their help, Crafty suddenly said, "Oh my God, my stamps!" He clapped his hand to his forehead in sudden panic.

"Stamps, sir?" Roy Grace asked.

Caroline Cunningham gave her husband an astonished look. "You didn't check, darling?"

"No… I… I… dammit, I didn't!"

"Where are they this week?"

Crafty looked bewildered for a moment. He stroked his chin.

"My husband's a stamp collector," Caroline explained. "But he's paranoid about them. Twenty-five years ago his collection was stolen – we always suspected the housekeeper had something to do with it because he kept them hidden in a particular place in his den, and the thieves went straight to it. Ever since, he's been paranoid – he changes the hiding place every few weeks."

"You don't use a safe, sir?" Roy Grace asked.

"Never trusted them," Crafty replied. "My parents had a safe in their house jemmied open. I prefer my hiding places."

"I keep telling him he's bloody stupid," his wife said. "But he won't listen."

"What's the value of your collection, Mr Cunningham?" Bill Stoker asked.

"About one hundred thousand pounds," he said absently, scratching his head now, thinking. "I... I had them under the carpet beneath the dining table," he said. "But then I moved them... um... ah, yes, of course, of course! I remember!"

With the rest of them in tow, he hurried through an internal door into the integral double garage. A large, elderly Rover was parked in there, along with an assortment of tools and two lawnmowers, one sitting on top of a hessian mat. He pulled the mower back and, like an excited child, knelt and lifted the mat.

Then he looked up in utter disbelief. "They've gone," he said lamely, looking gutted. "They've gone."

Both detectives frowned. "You kept a hundred thousand pounds worth of stamps beneath an old mat in the garage?" Bill Stoker said, incredulously.

"They're sealed," he said. "And there's no damp in the garage."

"How easy would the stamps be to identify, sir?" Roy Grace asked.

"Very easy if someone tried to sell them as a single collection.

They're all British Colonial from the Victorian period and there are some very rare ones among them. But not so easy if they sold them individually or in strips."

"And you have them insured, sir?"

"Yes."

"No insurance stipulation about having them locked in a safe or a bank vault?"

He shook his head. "Only have to do that if the house is empty."

"Do you have any photographs of these stamps, Mr Cunningham?" Roy Grace asked.

"Yes, I do. I can make you a copy of the list the insurance company has."

"Thank you, sir," the young detective said. "That would be very helpful. We'll be organizing some house-to-house inquiries over the next few days."

Afterwards in the car, heading back to the police station, Roy Grace said, "Something doesn't feel right."

"About the Cunninghams?"

He nodded.

"He's dodgy," Bill Stoker said. "Well dodgy."

"I sensed something. Couldn't put my finger on it."

Stoker touched the tip of his nose. "Copper's nose. You'll develop it more as you get experience, old son. Follow your instincts and you won't often go wrong. He's been known to us for years, but no one's ever pinned anything on him."

"Known for what?"

"Handling."

"Stamps?"

The DS shook his head. "High-end antiques. But anytime we ever tried to nick him, he could always produce receipts. He's crafty, that one. I've talked to a few people who reckon he's got away with everything but murder over the years. A lot of coppers would like to see him behind bars." He shrugged. "But doesn't look like it's going to happen, does it? And now he's a sodding victim."

"Reckon that's genuine?"

He nodded. "You could see how upset the missus is. They've had the tables turned, all right. Mind you, you sodding deserve it if you leave a hundred grand's worth of stamps under a bleeding mat, right?"

Grace nodded thoughtfully, replaying the scene over in his mind.

"The timing bothers me, sir – why do it at 5 a.m.? Why not earlier in the night?"

"Police patrols get suspicious of vehicles out late at night. If the Cunninghams are correct and the villains broke in at 5 a.m., did their burgling, then made themselves some breakfast, it meant they were probably there a good hour or so. They'd have left around 6 a.m. perhaps, when people are starting to surface and be up and about. More vehicles on the road. Less suspicion. Nah, it's an open-and-shut job. Let's see if SOCO pick up any dabs." He glanced at his watch. "They'll be there in the next half hour. We need to brief our press officer in the meantime. I'll let you do it – be good practice."

■ ■ ■

Shortly after 12.30 p.m., Tony Langiotti left his office, pulled his door shut behind him, a fresh cigarette dangling from his lips, and sauntered out into the bright sunshine. He was in a sunny mood, looking forward to a nice pint or two and a bite to eat in the pub with a couple of mates.

He'd already made a deal this morning to offload the Georgian silver haul from last night, for a very tasty price indeed! The clock wasn't proving quite so easy and he wished the tossers hadn't bothered nicking it – the value was peanuts compared to the rest of the items. But he knew someone who would take it off his hands when he returned from a holiday in Spain later in the week.

He climbed into his large Jaguar, started the engine, and drove up to the Old Shoreham Road. A short distance on he halted at a red traffic light. As he waited for it to change, he glanced idly towards the parade of shops on his left; suddenly, the banner headline of *The Argus* newspaper, outside a newsagent's, caught his eye.

Instantly, his mood darkened. Violently. It was too coincidental to be a different house.

"What?" he said aloud. "What?" he repeated. "What the f—?"

£100,000
STAMP HAUL IN EXCLUSIVE HOVE MANSION RAID

Ignoring that the lights had changed to green, and the hooting from behind, he sat and stared in disbelief for several moments. Then he jumped out, gave two fingers to the driver of the car behind, ran into the newsagent's and grabbed a copy of the paper. He paid for it, then stood rooted to the spot reading it, ignoring the hooting outside from the obstruction his car was causing.

> Thieves broke into a Dyke Road Avenue mansion early this morning And made off with a haul that included Georgian silver, valued at over £50,000, and a prized stamp collection, worth an estimated £100,000.
>
> The house's owner, retired Brighton businessman Dennis Cunningham, said to The Argus

earlier this morning, "They clearly knew exactly what they were looking for. They only targeted our finest Georgian silver – and my stamps. And the cheek of them!" he added, indignantly. "They helped themselves to breakfast while my wife and I were asleep upstairs!"

Detective Constable Roy Grace, in charge of the investigation, said, "We are pursuing a number of lines of enquiry, and will make every effort to apprehend those responsible and recover the valuables, many of which are of great sentimental value to their rightful owners.

> "If any member of the public saw anything suspicious in the Dyke Road Avenue area between the hours of 4 a.m. and 7 a.m., please call Detective Constable Roy Grace at Brighton CID on the following number..."

Langiotti stormed out of the newsagent, jumped into his car, lit another cigarette to calm himself down, then accelerated away, his lunchtime plans out of the window, anger coursing through his veins.

"Bastards," he said. "You jammy little Welsh bastards. Think you're going to get away with cheating me out of a hundred grand? Well, boyos, you've got another think coming."

■ ■ ■

In the CID office at John Street police station, Roy Grace was hunched over his desk, an untouched sandwich beside him and a forgotten mug of coffee gone cold. He was concentrating hard, determined to impress Detective Sergeant Stoker with his work on this case. And he knew he was going to impress one person today – his beloved Sandy. The noon edition of *The Argus* lay beside him; it was the first time he had ever seen his name in print, and he was chuffed to bits. He could not wait to show it to her this evening.

In his notebook he wrote:

– Look for similar modus operandi.

– House-to-house enquiries.

– Newsagents.

- Stop all vehicles in Dyke Road Avenue during that time period tomorrow and ask if they saw anything.

- Check all antique shops and stalls in Brighton regularly over coming weeks.

- Check local and national stamp dealers for items they have been offered.

He was interrupted in mid-flow by his phone ringing. "DC Grace," he answered. "Brighton CID."

"I'm phoning about the Dyke Road Avenue robbery this morning," the male voice at the other end said, in a coarse Brighton accent.

Eagerly, Grace picked up his pen.

"May I have your name and phone number, sir?"

"You may not. But I've got inside information, see. There's going to be another burglary tonight. 111 Tongdean Avenue, a house called The Gallops."

Grace knew his home town well. This was considered by some to be an even smarter street than Dyke Road Avenue. "How do you know that, sir?"

"Just trust me, I know. They'll be going in around 5 a.m., and coming out soon after 6 a.m., disguised as postmen. Couple of Welshmen, from Cardiff."

Any moment there was going to be a catch; Grace pressed on with his questions, whilst waiting for it. Probably a demand for money.

"Can you give me their names, sir?"

"Dai Lewellyn and Rees Hughes."

He wrote the names on the pad. "May I ask why you are giving me this information?"

"Tell 'em they shouldn't have been so greedy with the stamps."

There was a click. The man had hung up.

Grace thought for some moments, feeling a buzz of excitement. If... if... if this tip-off was real, then he had a real chance to shine! Even better if he could catch the perps red-handed. But it could of course have been a crank call. He phoned the operator and asked for a trace on it, then he looked up the number of Cardiff's main police station, called it, and asked to speak to the CID there. The duty detective was out at lunch, but Grace was told he would call back on his return.

A short while later the operator called to tell him the call had been made, as he had suspected, from a phone booth. She gave him the address of the booth, in a busy street near the Brighton & Hove Albion football stadium. Grace thanked her and immediately contacted the SOCO officer who had just finished at the Cunninghams' house, asking him to get straight over to the phone box and take some prints from that – although Grace doubted whether whoever had made the call would have been dumb enough to have left any prints anywhere in the booth.

Then he hurried across the room to Bill Stoker's tiny office, which was largely decorated with photographs of him in his former life as a professional boxer, and told him the developments.

"Probably a crank," was the Detective Sergeant's first reaction.

"He was very specific."

"Let's wait and see if Cardiff Police come back with anything on these two Taffies."

An hour later, Grace received a call from Detective Constable Gareth Brangwen of the South Wales Constabulary. Before getting down to business he asked whether Grace was a football or a rugby man. "I'm a rugby man, sir," he said, "Out of preference."

"Good man!" he said. "We're going to get along fine, you and I! Now, what's this about two of our undesirables over on your manor?"

The young DC gave him, as briefly as he could, the facts.

"Well, we do have a Dai Lewellyn and Rees Hughes well known to us. They come from the same estate and they've given us plenty of trouble over the years. Housebreaking is their speciality, if you want to call it that. Both of them have form – they were last released from prison six months ago."

Grace thanked him, hardly able to wait to give Bill Stoker the news.

■ ■ ■

There were several cars parked along both sides of Tongdean Avenue, so another one, a large plain Vauxhall, did not look out of place. Taking no chances, Roy Grace and another DC colleague, Jon Carlton, had arrived shortly before midnight for the stake-out.

they were parked across the road, a safe distance back from The Gallops, number 111, the target house. A quarter of a mile away, down a side street, other officers waited in an unmarked van. A second unmarked car, with two police officers seated inside, was parked in the street near the rear of the property. No one could go in or out without being seen from one of the roads.

There were to be no breaks, and no one leaving or entering any of the vehicles. If anyone, including Grace and Carlton, needed to urinate for the rest of the night, they'd have to do it into plastic jars, which they had with them.

One of the biggest decisions that had been made, fortunately by his superiors – so there would be no comeback on him at least – was not to inform the owners of The Gallops. The news would undoubtedly worry, if not downright terrify them. There would be no telling how the owners might react – perhaps by keeping the lights on all night long, which could blow the police's chances of an arrest. The plan was to seize the perpetrators as they attempted to enter the house.

Grace was nervous as hell – so much was riding on this. Would they turn up, or would he have wasted hours of time for eight officers, and DS Stoker, who had also sacrificed his night's sleep to be on standby for him? He'd have a very red face if there was a no-show, or if it all went, as Bill Stoker had charmingly put it, tits-up.

Grace wondered if he was noticing a pattern. The Gallops, which he had driven past in daylight earlier, was one of the largest houses in this street, but – like the Cunninghams' house – one of the ones in poorest repair, and there was no burglar alarm box on the wall. There were also no gates to the entrance or exit of the in-and-out driveway.

His colleague was an experienced and chatty DC, who was hoping to move across to Major Crime work, which included all homicides. High-profile murder cases were the best jobs, the *Gucci jobs,* he told Roy Grace over several cigarettes, which they smoked cupped in their hands to conceal the glow in case their quarry approached unseen, and sickly sweet coffee that was becoming progressively more lukewarm. They were also the cases that got you noticed by your superiors, and which helped your promotion chances.

As the night wore on, it wasn't promotion that was Grace's worry, it was his growing fear of a no-show. Had he been sold a pup? Been naive in believing a crank caller?

But the names of the two Welshmen had checked out, hadn't they? If it had been a crank call, whoever had made it had gone to a lot of trouble.

At a few minutes past five, DC Carlton yawned. "What time are you reckoning on calling it a day?"

The sky was lightening a fraction, Grace thought, and a few tiny streaks of grey and red were appearing. He felt tired, and shaky from too much coffee. He munched a Kit Kat chocolate bar, sharing it with Carlton. Then, just as he bit on the last morsel, both men stiffened.

Headlights appeared.

A white van drove slowly past them, with what looked like two men in the front. All the cars parked on this street, and on the driveways of the homes, were modern; this Vauxhall they were in was one of the cheapest, but it was inconspicuous. The van stuck out instantly. The vehicle was wrong for the street – certainly at this hour.

Grace radioed in. "Charlie Victor, Tango One approaching Tango Two."

But the van carried on going and Grace's heart sank. Then it turned around and came back, and pulled into a space less than a hundred yards in front of them. Two men climbed out. In the glow of a street light he could see they were dressed as postmen, carrying what looked like empty mail sacks. They looked furtively around at the seemingly deserted street, then scurried across the road, hurried along the pavement and down the driveway.

"Now," he radioed urgently. "Tango One on scene. Charlie Victor going in. Unit Two, move forward!"

Grace signalled to his colleague to wait for a few more seconds, pulled his torch out of the glove compartment without switching it on, then as quietly as they could, they slipped out of the car and hurried across the road. The driveway of The Gallops was tarmac, and on their rubber-soled shoes they made little noise as they hurried around the side of the house. Then they stopped.

Right in front of them, barely twenty feet ahead, they saw the silhouettes of the two men. Then they heard a tinkle of glass. In the distance, Grace heard the roar of an engine being revved hard. He snapped on his torch, lighting up their startled faces, and yelled, "Police, don't move!" as both officers sprinted forwards.

"Shite!" One of the thieves shouted, dropping his tools and making a run for it across the lawn. Grace broke away to the right, sprinting hard to try to cut him off. Out of the corner of his eyes he saw the other trying to climb the wall into the neighbour's garden and being dragged back down by Carlton. But all his focus was on the sprinting man ahead of him. Gripping his torch, the beam jigging everywhere, Grace was gaining on him on the damp grass. Gaining. Then suddenly his quarry appeared to trip and plunge forward in the darkness. An instant later, as the ground gave way beneath him, he realized why.

For an instant he swayed wildly, then fell forward too, the torch rolling away from him onto the soft, tensioned cover of the swimming pool. He reached forward and grabbed an ankle, as the thief attempted to scramble away. Grace clung to it, as the Welshman kicked hard and swore, then moments later he broke free, leaving Grace floundering on the material, now sodden with chlorinated water, holding a trainer in his hand. He lurched to his feet, and stumbled forward through ankle-deep water, radioing for assistance.

Ahead he saw the Welshman haul himself back onto terra firma and sprint towards the end of the garden. Not bothering to pick up his torch, Grace sprinted on after him. Suddenly, appearing to change his mind, the thief turned and ran back towards the house, and seconds later was lit up by the beams of three different torches. He stopped in his tracks. Before he knew it he was face down on the ground, with two officers on top of him.

"Out for an early morning stroll are we, sunshine?" said one.

"Bit careless forgetting a shoe when you got dressed, wasn't it?" said the other. "Got any mail for us then?"

■ ■ ■

Back at the police station, ignoring his Sergeant's advice to go home and get some dry clothes and some kip, Grace insisted on going down into the custody block in the basement. Dai Lewellyn and Rees Hughes had been read their rights, and were now locked in separate cells, still dressed as postmen, waiting for a duty Legal Aid solicitor to arrive.

Grace, his tie awry, his clothes sodden, walked through the custody centre in the basement of the police station and peered through one of the cell doors. "Got everything you need?"

Lewellyn looked at him sullenly. "So, how did you know?"

"Know what?"

"You know what I mean. You knew we were coming, didn't you? Someone grassed us up, didn't they?"

Grace raised his eyebrows. "A little bird told me you shouldn't have been so greedy with the stamps. That mean anything?"

"Stamps?" Lewellyn said. "What do you

mean, *stamps*? We didn't have no stamps. You mean, like in postage stamps?"

"Yes."

"I don't know what you're talking about. We didn't take no stamps. Why would we take stamps? I don't know nothing about no stamps."

"But you and your mate know all about Georgian silver?" Grace asked.

Lewellyn was silent for some moments. "We might," he said finally. "But not stamps." He was emphatic.

"Someone thinks you've been greedy over stamps."

"I don't understand," Lewellyn said. "Who?"

"A man who knows where you were yesterday and what you took."

"There's only one bastard who knows where we was," he said, even more emphatically.

Roy Grace listened attentively.

■ ■ ■

The next two hours were taken up with formal interviews with the two men. In the end they admitted the burglary, but continued to deny any involvement with stamps, and indeed any knowledge of them.

Finally, shortly before 10 a.m., still in his damp clothes, with a search warrant signed by a local magistrate in his hand, along with the inventory folder and photographs of the valuables taken and a fresh team of officers, Grace arrived at

West Southwick Mews. Their pissed-off co-operative Welsh prisoners had kindly supplied them with the exact address.

One officer broke the door down with the yellow battering ram, and they entered, found the switch and turned the lights on. They were in a huge space, eight garages wide, and almost empty, bar a row of trestle tables – and what looked to Grace like a rather ugly antique clock.

Five minutes later, Tony Langiotti arrived for the start of his day, in his Jaguar, cigarette as ever dangling between his lips. As he drove into the mews and saw the police officers, he stamped on the brakes, and frantically threw the gear shift into reverse. But before he could touch the accelerator a police car appeared from nowhere, completely blocking off the exit behind him.

The cigarette fell from his lips and it took him several seconds to realize. By then it was burning his crotch.

■ ■ ■

There was not such a big hurry for Roy Grace's last call of what was turning out to be a very long day or, rather, extended day. It was 2 p.m. and he'd had no sleep since yesterday. But he was running on an adrenaline high – helped by a lot of caffeine. So far everything had gone to plan – well, in truth, he had to admit, somewhat better than planned. Three in custody, and, if he was right, by the close of play there would be four. But, he knew, it might not be such an easy task to convince DS Stoker.

He went home to shower and change, wolf down some cereal and toast and to think his next – potentially dangerous – step through. If he was wrong, it could be highly embarrassing, not to mention opening the police up to a possible lawsuit. But he did not think he was wrong. He was increasingly certain, as his next bout of tiredness waned, that he was right. But speed again might be of the essence.

Whether it was because he was impressed with his results to date, or it gave him the chance to settle an old, unresolved score, DS Bill Stoker agreed to Grace's request far more readily than he had expected, although to cover his back, he still wanted to run it by the Detective Inspector. He in turn decided to run it by the Chief Superintendent, who was out at a meeting.

■ ■ ■

Finally, shortly after 5 p.m., running on his second, or maybe even third or fourth wind, Roy Grace had all his ducks in a row. Accompanied by DS Stoker, who was looking as weary as Grace felt, he pulled up in the street outside the Cunninghams' house. A van, with trained search officers, pulled up behind, and they all climbed out.

Roy Grace and Stoker walked up to the front door. Grace held in his hand his second document signed by a magistrate today. He rang the bell and waited. A few moments later, it was opened by the old man. He looked at them, and the entourage behind them, with a puzzled frown. "Good afternoon, officers," he said. "To what do I owe this pleasure? Do you have some news for me?"

"We have some good news and some bad news, Mr Cunningham," Roy Grace said. "The good news is we believe we have recovered your stolen clock."

"Nothing else?"

"Not so far, sir, but we have made some arrests and we are hopeful of recovering further items."

"Well, that's good. So what's the bad news?"

"I have a warrant to search these premises, sir." Grace showed him the signed warrant.

"What exactly is this about?"

"I think you know that, sir," he said with a tired smile.

■ ■ ■

Trained police search teams, Roy Grace learned rapidly, missed few things. Not that the stamps had been hidden in a difficult place to find – they were beneath a crate of Champagne in the cupboard under the stairs that served as the Cunninghams' wine cellar.

But it was three other items they found that were really to seal Crafty's fate. The first was an insurance claim form that lay on his desk, faxed only this morning, but which he had already started to fill out with details of the missing stamps.

The second was another fax, lying beneath it, to a dealer in the US, offering the collection for sale to him.

The third was a fax back from the US dealer, offering slightly more than the £100,000 Crafty had given the detectives as an estimate.

■ ■ ■

Later that night, even though he was exhausted, Roy Grace insisted on taking Sandy out to dinner to celebrate the first highly successful days of his new post, rather than going to the bar with the other officers. Four arrests! "We got lucky," he said. "If the Chief Superintendent hadn't been out, and delayed us for several hours, and we had gone early, he might not have started filling in that insurance form. He might not have sent that damning fax. And he might not have had the damning reply." He pulled out the folded page from *The Argus* newspaper and showed it to her.

She read it then smiled at him. "I'm very proud of you." She raised her wine glass, and clinked it against his, and said with another smile, this one a tad wistful, "Now, how about asking me about my day?"

About the Author

Peter James is a UK No.1 bestselling author, best known for his Detective Superintendent Roy Grace series, now a hit ITV drama starring John Simm as the troubled Brighton copper.

Peter has won over 40 awards and to date has written an impressive total of 19 *Sunday Times* No. 1s, sold over 21 million copies worldwide and been translated into 38 languages. His books are also often adapted for the stage – the most recent being *Looking Good Dead*.

Also by Peter James

Roy Grace Detective Series

Dead Simple
Looking Good Dead
Not Dead Enough
Dead Man's Footsteps
Dead Tomorrow
Dead Like You
Dead Man's Grip
Not Dead Yet
Dead Man's Time
Want You Dead
You Are Dead
Love You Dead
Need You Dead
Dead If You Don't
Dead At First Sight
Find Them Dead
Left You Dead
Wish You Were Dead
Picture You Dead

Other Novels

Dead Letter Drop	The Truth
Atom Bomb Angel	Denial
Billionaire	Faith
Travelling Man	The Perfect Murder (novella)
Biggles: The Untold Story	Perfect People
Possession	A Twist of the Knife (short story collection)
Dreamer	
Sweet Heart	The House on Cold Hill
Twilight	
Prophecy	Absolute Proof
Host	The Secret of Cold Hill
Alchemist	
Getting Wired	I Follow You

**More dyslexic friendly
titles coming soon...**

BOTH
PUBLISHING

Ingram Content Group UK Ltd.
Milton Keynes UK
UKHW040633220523
422126UK00004B/28